This book belongs to

_____

This edition published by Parragon in 2011

Parragon
Queen Street House
4 Queen Street
Bath BA1 1HE, UK
www.parragon.com

Copyright © 2011 Disney Enterprises, Inc.

ISBN 978-1-4075-8912-1

Printed in China

The Prince & the Pauper

Bath · New York · Singapore · Hong Kong · Cologne · Delhi
Melbourne · Amsterdam · Johannesburg · Auckland · Shenzhen

Once upon a time, there was a kingdom ruled over by a good and kindly king. But one day, the king fell ill and could no longer watch over his land. His son, the Prince, watched anxiously by his father's bedside. What would happen to the kingdom if the king died?

Elsewhere in the kingdom, there lived a pauper, Mickey, and his two friends, the bumbling Goofy and Pluto, his friendly dog. It just so happened that Mickey looked exactly like the Prince, although he did not know it.

On that particular day, Mickey and his friends were so hungry they were trying to sell fake ice creams to get money for food.

Just then a coach sped by. Mickey and Goofy watched as the evil captain of the guards sped by in the royal coach, which was overflowing with delicious food.

"Woof, woof," barked the hungry Pluto as he chased the coach towards the palace.

"Stop!" cried Mickey. "Come back!" He dashed after Pluto.

Pluto chased the royal coach to the gates of the palace, with Mickey following close behind him. To Mickey's surprise, the royal guard bowed deeply to him and let him right through! He even called him "Your Majesty"…

"Our prince is certainly dressed oddly today," thought the guard.

By now, Goofy had lost sight of Mickey and wondered where he and Pluto had got to.

Suddenly, the captain was standing behind the guard who had let Mickey through the gates.

"You fool!" shouted the captain, grabbing the guard. "Can't you see that the real prince is in his study?"

The captain pointed up at a window. Mickey looked up too and there in a high window he saw a shadow which looked strangely similar to his own.

Meanwhile, inside the palace, the real prince was sitting through a very boring lesson. To amuse himself, he took out his peashooter and aimed it at his servant, Donald.

"Wak!" cried Donald when he got hit.

The prince had all the food he could want and lots of fine clothes, but he often wished he could explore the world beyond the palace.

When the prince heard a loud din outside, he opened the window and looked out in order to see what was going on. The Captain had picked Mickey up by the collar and was about to throw Mickey out onto the street.

This did not please the prince at all. Furiously he called to the captain, "You may not treat my subjects like this. Even the poorest creatures from my realm deserve respect. Please let him go at once."

So Mickey was released, and allowed to wander through the halls of the palace. He marvelled at all the lovely things he could see.

"Look how shiny this floor is!" he said to himself in wonder. "I can see my reflection in it!"

Mickey was so busy gazing around him that he walked right into some suits of armour, making an almighty crash! The prince darted out of his lesson to see what all the commotion was and saw the suits of armour wobbling dangerously!

Both Mickey and the prince ended up on the floor, each hidden by a suit of armour. They peered cautiously at each other from under their helmets.

"Who could this be?" they both wondered at the same time. They were both sure they had not met before, but there was something familiar about the other one...

They both took their helmets off at the same time...and they couldn't believe their eyes!

"We look the same!" both Mickey and the prince said at once!

They examined every inch of themselves, right up to the tips of their ears. There was no doubt about it – they were identical! Then the prince had an idea...

24

"How happy you must be," the Prince said to Mickey. "You are free to wander outside and play all day long."

"But you have lots of wonderful feasts and clothes," sighed the hungry Mickey.

"Why don't we change places for the day?" said the Prince, swapping hats with Mickey. "Being a prince is easy!"

Mickey thought this was an excellent idea and pretty soon they were wearing each other's clothes.

Disguised as Mickey the pauper, the prince sneaked out the window down to where the captain of the guards was standing. He waved to Mickey who was peeking out the window, wondering where on earth he would start to learn how to be a prince!

"Have fun!" said the prince.

The captain of the guards spotted the prince dressed as Mickey and he caught him.

"That'll teach you to trespass in the palace!" the evil guard said, as he catapulted the prince over the wall.

"Hee, hee!" laughed Mickey as he sailed over the wall. "Even my own guard didn't recognise me!"

The prince landed with a thump in the snow outside the palace grounds.

"Mickey!" shouted Goofy, delighted to see his old friend again. But Pluto, after a quick sniff, was a little suspicious.

As Goofy swept up the prince into a great big hug, Pluto walked away slowly, convinced that this wasn't their old friend after all.

The prince, who wasn't at all sure who this strange person was, wriggled in Goofy's grip, eager to start exploring the world outside the palace walls.

Inside the palace, Mickey had been given an enormous speech to learn for an upcoming ball.

"Phew!" thought Mickey, "being a prince sure is hard work!"

There were many royal tasks he had to do before the end of the day.

He was enjoying his fine new clothes, however, and more food than he had eaten in days!

Meanwhile, the prince was learning that even though he could wander around freely outside the palace, there were very hard things to learn – like how to win and a snowball fight...

... and how to get food!

He had found some leftover chicken, but as soon as he took a bit to eat, he was immediately chased by some hungry stray dogs.

In the palace, a science lesson was in full swing. Unfortunately for Donald, Mickey found out that he was a not a natural sceintist. An experiment went very wrong. Mickey caused an explosion which blew up in poor Donald's face.

Donald was not impressed at all as his face was turned completely black, and his ears smoked.

Meanwhile as the prince ran from the dogs, he suddenly stumbled across one of the palace guards, trying to take a chicken away from a poor peasant woman and her children.

"Hey!" cried Mickey, "Stop that at once!"

Ignoring the prince, the guard snatched the chicken and walked off laughing meanly with his friend.

"Hey," a small child said to the prince. "Thank you for trying to help us, but it won't do any good. The captain and all his guards are always stealing our food."

The prince couldn't believe that the guards had been stealing food from the poor people of the kingdom!

"I have to put a stop to this!" said the prince, and ran over to the royal food wagon.

The prince flashed his royal ring at the driver of the coach and the guards recognised him as the prince.

"I order you to give these people food!" the prince said.

All the people gathered round the prince as he passed out the food that they should have had all along.

"Once I get back to the palace there are a few changes I am going to make!" the prince said smiling, as he handed round the food to his people.

But the guards were not pleased with his generosity. They informed the captain that there was something very suspicious going on.

That same night, the prince found out that the king had passed away. Showing Goofy his ring, the prince revealed his true identity. He had to get to the palace for his coronation the next day.

Suddenly, the captain and his guards burst into the room! He had discovered that the prince and Mickey had swapped places.

"Your royal ring won't do you any good!" said the captain grabbing the prince, "It's the dungeon for you – and my chance to take control of the kingdom!"

When the captain arrived back at the palace he took the prince to the dungeons. On their way, they met Donald, who was overjoyed to be reunited with the true prince.
Donald's loyalty to the prince made the captain so angry that he locked him up as well!

The prince and Donald had to spend an uncomfortable night in the dungeon with a scary guard standing outside their cell; there was no way they could escape.

"Oh no!" cried the prince when they saw another scary-looking guard approaching. "How are we ever going to escape? If I don't get out in time for my coronation, our kingdom will be ruined!"

But then they noticed the guard did seem a little bumbly and clumsy. All of a sudden the guard lost his balance and hit the other guard on the head, making his mask fly off.

It was Goofy!

"You've rescued me again!" cried the prince. Donald quacked happily.

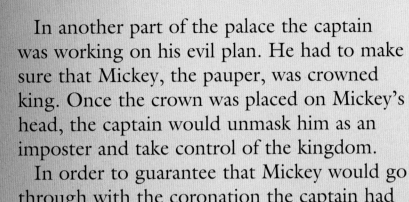

In another part of the palace the captain
was working on his evil plan. He had to make
sure that Mickey, the pauper, was crowned
king. Once the crown was placed on Mickey's
head, the captain would unmask him as an
imposter and take control of the kingdom.

In order to guarantee that Mickey would go
through with the coronation the captain had
kidnapped Pluto. The captain knew that Mickey
would not do anything to endanger Pluto.

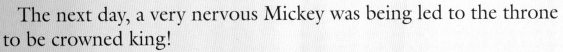

The next day, a very nervous Mickey was being led to the throne to be crowned king!

"What should I do?" worried Mickey, "and where is the real prince?"

The evil captain watched from the side door, with Pluto trapped by his ears so he couldn't sniff out his true friend Mickey and give the game away.

Just as the crown was being placed on his head Mickey ducked and shouted at the guards, "Stop! Arrest the captain, he is a villain!"

The captain approached the throne and shouted back, "He's an imposter! Seize him!"

"But I'm not an imposter!" a voice said from high above. Everyone gasped when they saw the real prince swinging down to them from a chandelier! There was a thrilling sword fight, as the prince bravely battled with the captain of the guards. Mickey watched from the throne, willing the prince on.

Just then, the chandelier that the prince had used to swing down on crashed on top of the guards, trapping them! The prince caught the evil captain's trousers on the tip of his sword.

"Eeek!" the captain squealed, and he ran away, never to return! Everyone cheered.

Finally, the true prince sat down on his throne and the crown was placed on his head. He was the king at last!

Mickey and all his friends bowed, happy that honour would be restored to the kingdom.

Everyone celebrated that night. Though they had enjoyed their adventures, the prince was happy to be back in his rightful place, and Mickey was just pleased to be reunited with his old pals Goofy and Pluto!